Book 1

The Magical Meteorite

written by

Tonya Flores

illustrated by Darrin Drda and Kira Reed

To my daughter, Jessica, who fills my life with sunshine.
And to her puppy, Zuko, who inspired this series of books.

Copyright © 2022 by Tonya Flores

TGF Books LLC
tonya@thesuperpuppies.com
www.thesuperpuppies.com

ISBN: 9798353894971

MEET THE PUPPIES

NAME: ZUKO
BREED: Mini pinscher
LIKES: Eating yummy stuff and playing
DISLIKES: Paying attention

NAME: ALLIE PUFF
BREED: Maltese
LIKES: Wearing bows and solving problems
DISLIKES: When others aren't paying attention

One beautiful spring day, two puppies named Zuko and Allie Puff were playing in the park.

"Woof! Woof! Woof!" Zuko barked around the ball in his mouth.

Allie Puff panted happily. She knew what that bark meant. Zuko wanted to play tag!

Allie Puff chased Zuko up and down hills and around trees. Finally, she caught up to him.

"Woof! Woof!" she barked, which meant "Got you!"

Tired from their game, Allie Puff sat down to rest. That's when she noticed a giant rock flying their way!

"Arf! Arf!" she warned.

Zuko whipped around and saw the rock hurtling toward them. Before he could let loose a single bark, the meteorite struck. The ground around them shook.

"Ruff! Ruff! Ruff! Ruff!" he barked, meaning "Let's check it out!"

Allie Puff wasn't so sure that was a good idea. But she didn't want to be left alone, either, so she trotted along behind Zuko.

Dark dust blew the puppies' way as they inched toward the meteorite.

Finally, Zuko let out a loud, excited bark. He had found the rock!

To the puppies' surprise, the meteorite had split open. A sparkling cube floated in the air above it, as if by magic.

Allie Puff's eyes grew wide. "Arf! Arf!" she barked, warning Zuko to be careful.

But Zuko couldn't be careful. A sweet scent was drifting from the cube, teasing his nose and making his tummy rumble.

Zuko jumped for the cube. "Ruff! Ruff! Ruff!" he barked.

Allie Puff knew that bark too. Winner takes all! With a bark of her own, she lunged for the cube.

The puppies reached the cube at the same time.

Zuko dug his teeth into
the white half, while Allie Puff
dug hers into the purple.

The puppies tugged furiously on the cube, each determined to win it. Suddenly, the sweet cube split in half.

The puppies flew back and landed on their bottoms, each with their own piece of the cube.

Zuko and Allie Puff wasted no time. They each bit into their piece.

The cube halves exploded in their mouths like fireworks on the Fourth of July!

Zuko's eyes grew wider as what felt like an electrical current passed through his body!

Beside him, Allie Puff's ears pointed out straighter, and she felt something just as strange happening in her brain!

"What was that?" Allie Puff asked. Then she stopped, alarmed. "Whoa. I can talk?"

Without thinking, Zuko replied, "Sounds like it. Hey, I can talk too!"

Allie Puff stared at a flower. "Check this out!" She giggled. "I can make it grow as big as a tree!"

Suddenly, a butterfly flew past Zuko's tail. He lunged for it, only to find himself spinning in circles faster than he ever had before.

"Did you see that?" he asked.

As Allie Puff looked toward him, she noticed a sign. "Look, Zuko, we're next to a butterfly garden!" she said. "Wait . . . I can read that sign?"

Confused, Allie Puff lay down to take a break. But her mind couldn't rest. All sorts of knowledge was whipping around her brain: things like math and science—including how to make objects that fly!

A bird flew past Zuko, and he jumped to catch it. "Wow!" he shouted as his body soared up into the air.

He could fly!

"Whatever that cube was, it gave us superpowers!" Zuko shouted excitedly.

Allie Puff agreed. "Now all we need are superhero costumes!"

The two puppies chatted happily as they ran home. They didn't even notice the two tiny Chihuahuas hovering above them, watching their every move.

Back in the doghouse, Allie Puff designed their superhero costumes.

She even made herself
an advanced technology
jet pack so she could
fly around with Zuko.

"Wow!" Allie Puff said as the super puppies checked themselves out in the mirror. "We really look like superheroes now!"

Zuko let out a yawn. "Yeah, but all that excitement today made me sleepy."

Allie Puff agreed. They could be superheroes another day.

Now it was time for super sleeping and the best dreams ever.

What's next for these super puppies?

Another amazing adventure—guaranteed!

THIS BOOK BELONGS TO
_ _ _ _ _ _ _ _
_ _ _ _ _ _ _
_ _ _ _ _ _ _

Printed in Great Britain
by Amazon